TiGER CAN'T SLEEP

by **S. J. Fore**

illustrated by **R. W. Alley**

SCHOLASTIC INC.
New York Toronto London Auckland Sydney
Mexico City New Delhi Hong Kong Buenos Aires

To my mother and father, for their lifelong encouragement and support.
And with eternal gratitude to my editor, Janet B. Pascal.—S.J.F.

For Aunt Norma, who has many closets, all equally fun.—R.W.A.

ISBN-13: 978-0-545-06181-0
ISBN-10: 0-545-06181-4

12 11 10 9 8 7 6 5 4 3   9 10 11 12/0

Printed in the U.S.A.   40

First Scholastic printing, December 2007

Set in Typeka

Book design by Nancy Brennan

Cozy bed . . . time to sleep.

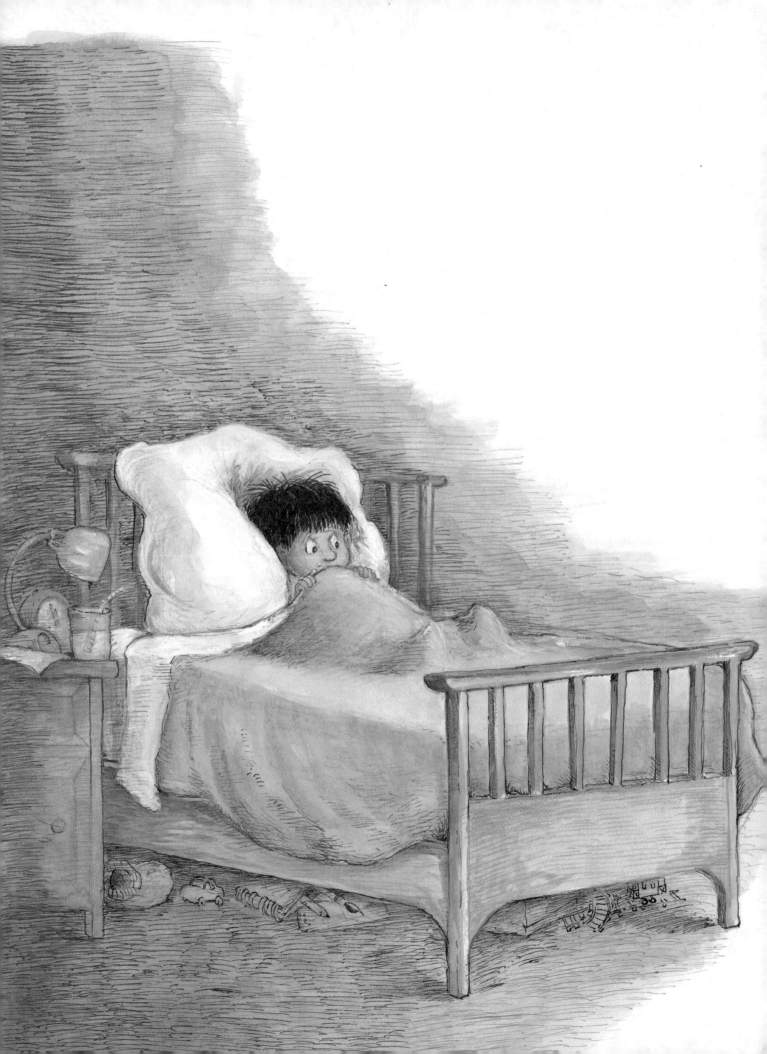

But I **can't** sleep
because there's a tiger
in my closet . . .

...a tiger in my closet eating potato chips!

Crunch! Crunch! CRUNCH!

"Shhh! Will you please be quiet in there?
I'm trying to sleep," I tell the tiger.

"Oops! Tiger is sorry.
Tiger will be quiet,"
the tiger says.

Everything is quiet.

I try to sleep.

Then I hear . . .

"Shhh! Didn't you hear me?
I'm trying to sleep!
Will you please be quiet in there?"

"Oops! Tiger is sorry.
Tiger will be quiet now,"
the tiger says.

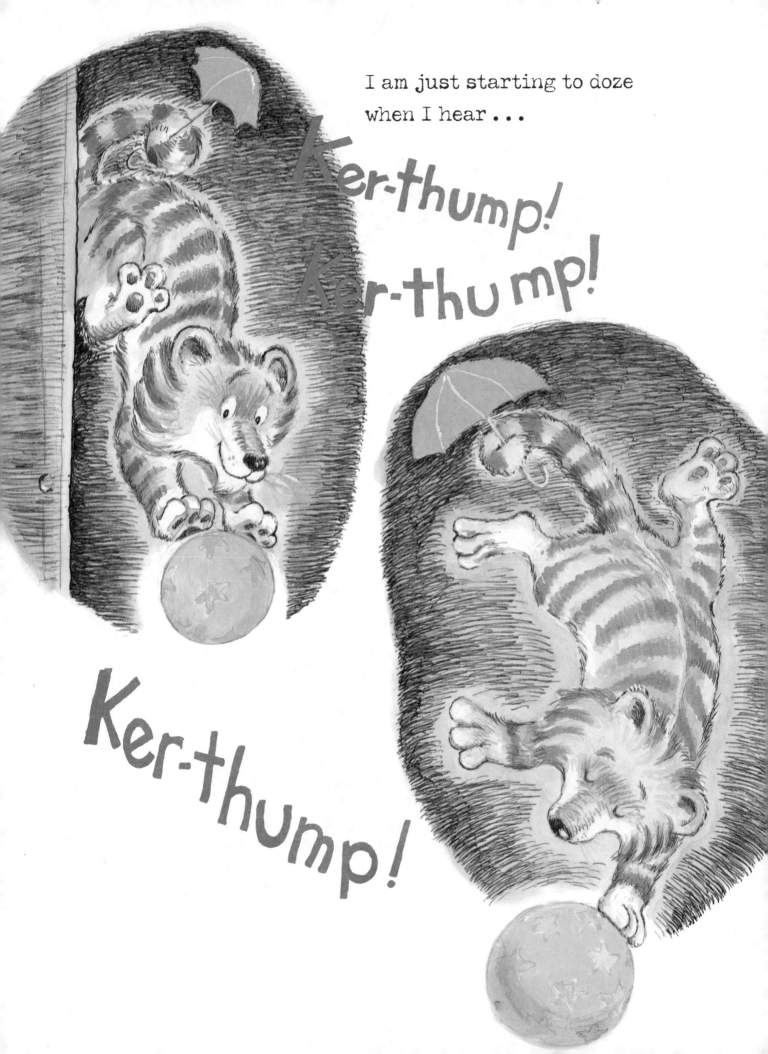

I am just starting to doze
when I hear . . .

Ker-thump!

Ker-thump!

Ker-thump!

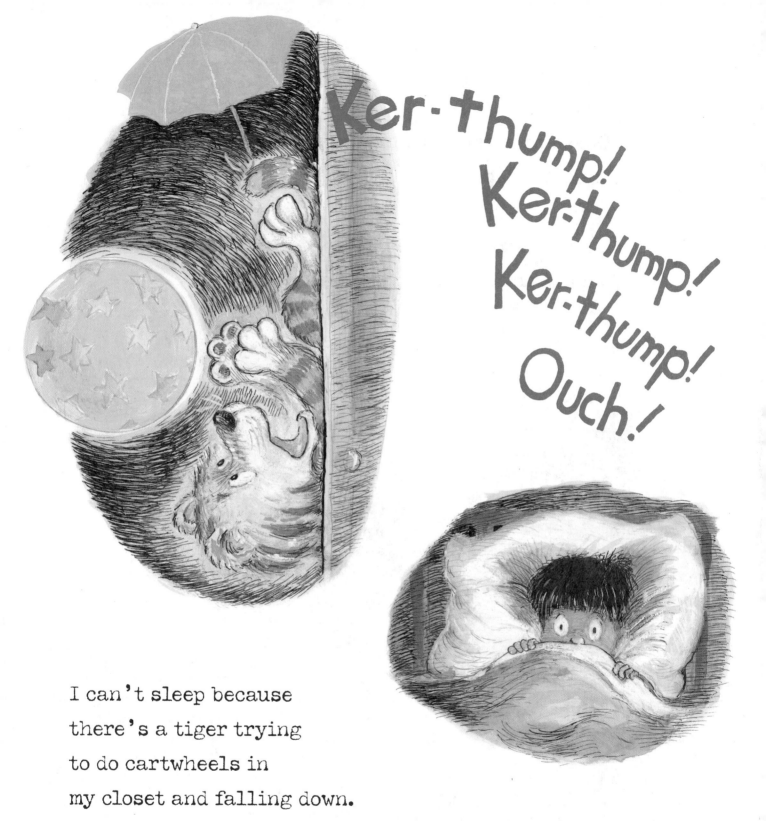

Ker-thump! Ker-thump! Ker-thump! Ouch!

I can't sleep because there's a tiger trying to do cartwheels in my closet and falling down.

My eyes pop open.

"Shhhh!
Please be quiet in there. I can't sleep!"
I tell the tiger.

"And no more cartwheels!
You are going to hurt yourself."

"**Oops!** Tiger is sorry. Tiger won't make another sound."

The tiger stops ker-thumping and ouching, and
everything is quiet again.

I try to sleep.

But it's impossible to sleep when you have a
talented tiger in your closet. . . .

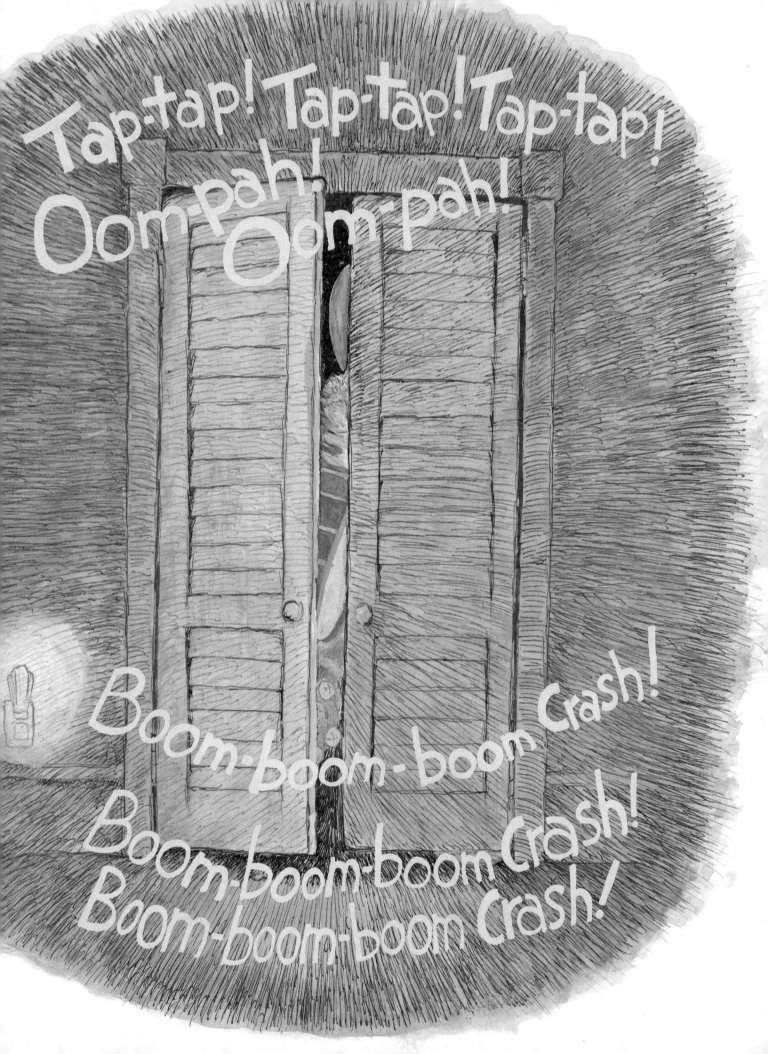

"Shhh, Tiger!

Quiet!

You are driving me crazy!
I'm trying to sleep. I don't want to hear
any more noise.
No tapping. No tuba playing.
No drumming. Not one more single noise!"

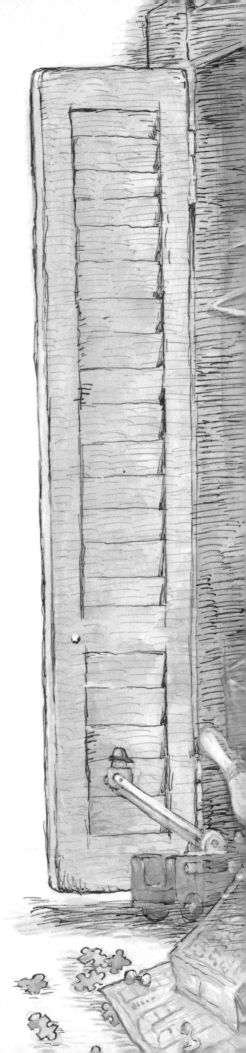

"**Oops!** Tiger is sorry.
Tiger will be very, very quiet,"
the tiger says.

But I don't listen to the tiger
this time.
I take the drum and cymbals
away from him.
I grab the potato chips,
   the ball,
      the tap shoes,
       the banjo,
     and the tuba.

"Now NO MORE NOISE!"

I march back to bed and climb in. Everything is quiet.

Maybe the tiger has finally stopped making noise. I try to sleep. Then I hear ...

Click-clack!
Click-clack!
Click-clack!

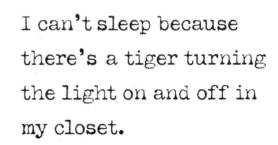

I can't sleep because there's a tiger turning the light on and off in my closet.

"Tiger!

That does it!
STOP! Don't
make me come back
over there!"

"Oops! Tiger is sorry.
Please don't be mad!
Tiger will be quiet
from now on. Promise,"
the tiger says.

The light stops click-
clacking. Everything is
quiet again.

I listen. I listen harder.
I don't hear a thing.
Everything is quiet for one minute.
Everything is quiet for two minutes.
Everything is quiet for three minutes.
I wonder what the tiger is doing now.
Maybe the tiger is asleep.
Then . . .

"Why are you crying?"
I ask the tiger.

"It's dark in this closet. Tiger is scared," the
tiger says. "Can Tiger sleep in your bed?"

"Um ... okay," I say.

Tiger hurries out of the closet, runs across my
room, jumps into my bed, gives me a big kiss, closes
his eyes, and pulls the covers over his head.

I close my eyes, too, and listen.
I listen harder. I keep listening. I
don't hear a thing.

I don't hear any **crunch-crunch-crunching.**

I don't hear any **bounce-bounce-bouncing.**

I don't hear any **ker-thump-thump, ouching.**

I don't hear any **tap-tap-tap-tapping.**

I don't hear any **oom-pah, oom-pahing.**

I don't hear any **boom-boom-boom-crashing.**

I don't hear any **click-clack, click-clacking.**

I don't even hear any **boo-hoo-hooing.**

Everything is quiet.

Now I'll finally be able to sleep!

Suddenly I hear a noise coming from under
the covers.

It gets louder and louder...
and louder.

I can't sleep
because there's a
tiger snoring in my bed.